This book belongs to

LADYBIRD BOOKS

UK | USA | Canada | Ireland | Australia | India | New Zealand | South Africa

Ladybird Books is part of the Penguin Random House group of companies
whose addresses can be found at global.penguinrandomhouse.com.

www.penguin.co.uk   www.puffin.co.uk   www.ladybird.co.uk

Penguin
Random House
UK

First published 2021
001

Licensed by

Hasbro   eOne

Printed in the United Kingdom by Print 4 Limited

The authorized representative in the EEA is Penguin Random House Ireland,
Morrison Chambers, 32 Nassau Street, Dublin D02 YH68

A CIP catalogue record for this book is available from the British Library

ISBN: 978–0–241–54891–2

All correspondence to:
Ladybird Books, Penguin Random House Children's
One Embassy Garder's, 8 Viaduct Gardens, London SW11 7BW

MIX
Paper from
responsible sources
FSC
www.fsc.org
FSC® C018179

Peppa Gets a Vaccination

Mummy Pig was taking Peppa to the doctor
for her health check and vaccination.
"Are we all ready?" said Mummy Pig.
"Yes!" said Peppa. "I've got Teddy."

"And *I've* got your red book," added Mummy Pig.
"What's that?" asked Peppa.
"It's your very own book," said Mummy Pig. "It helps doctors to see how you're growing up."

"Hello, Peppa," said Dr Brown Bear when they arrived. "Have you come for your health check and vaccination?"

"Yes!" said Peppa. "I've brought my red book and Teddy, too!"
"Very good," replied Dr Brown Bear.
"You're seeing Dr Polar Bear today."

Suddenly, a bell rang. *Ding!*

"Ahhh, that means she's ready to
see you," explained Dr Brown Bear.

Peppa and Mummy Pig walked into the doctor's office.
"Hello," said Dr Polar Bear cheerily. "Who do we have here?"
"I'm Peppa," said Peppa, "and this is Teddy."

"Lovely," said Dr Polar Bear. "Now, did you bring your red book?"
Peppa handed her book to Dr Polar Bear.
"Excellent!" said Dr Polar Bear.

"Let's start by seeing how tall you are," said Dr Polar Bear.
She took Peppa over to the measuring stick. Peppa stood up
very straight.
"Wonderfully done," said Dr Polar Bear.

"I'm a big girl now," Peppa said proudly.
"Yes, you are," said Dr Polar Bear. She got out her pen and wrote Peppa's height in the red book.

"Now, Peppa . . . can you hop on these for me, please?" said Dr Polar Bear, pointing to her weighing scales.
Peppa stepped on to the scales.

Clink!
Clank!

"These scales tell us how heavy you are,"
said Dr Polar Bear.
"Oooh," said Peppa.
"That's good," said Dr Polar Bear, writing in
Peppa's red book again.

"Now it's time to use a stethoscope to listen to your heart," said Dr Polar Bear.

"What's a setty-coat?" asked Peppa.

"A *stethoscope* helps me hear your heartbeat and the air going in and out of your lungs," said Dr Polar Bear. "I put this bit on your chest and listen through the earpieces."

Bumpy-dump!
Bumpy-dump!
Bumpy-dump!

"Peppa," said Dr Polar Bear, "would **you** like to listen to your heart beating?"
"Yes, please!" cried Peppa.

Dr Polar Bear put the stethoscope's earpieces on Peppa's ears.
"Hee! Hee!" said Peppa. "It's going *bumpy-dump, bumpy-dump, bumpy-dump!*"

Bumpy-dump!
Bumpy-dump!
Bumpy-dump!

"Now it's **your** turn, Teddy!" said Peppa, putting the stethoscope's chest piece on Teddy's chest. "Is Teddy's heart going *bumpy-dump, bumpy-dump, bumpy-dump*?" asked Dr Polar Bear.

"No," said Peppa. "Teddy's heart doesn't do that, because Teddy is a toy."
"Oh. I see," said Dr Polar Bear, smiling.

Next, Dr Polar Bear got out her special doctor's torch.
"I'm going to look in your ears now," she said.

Dr Polar Bear shone the torch into each of Peppa's ears.

Hee!
Hee!

"Hee! Hee!" said Peppa. "That tickles!"
Dr Polar Bear checked carefully inside Peppa's ears.
"That all looks lovely," she said.

"Now I'll check your mouth," said Dr Polar Bear.
"I need you to open wide and say *Ahhhh!*"
Dr Polar Bear opened her mouth and showed Peppa
what to do. "Like this . . . *Ahhhh!*"

Ahhhh!

Peppa opened her mouth as wide as it would
go and stuck her tongue out. "*AHHHHHHH!*"
she yelled **very** loudly.
"Wonderful!" said Dr Polar Bear.

"Do you want to check my nose?" asked Peppa.
"*SNOORRRTTTT!*"
"Ha! Ha! Thank you, Peppa," said Dr Polar Bear.
"I can see that your nose is working **very** well!"

Everyone laughed. "Hee! Hee! Hee!" Dr Polar Bear put lots of ticks in Peppa's red book.

Hee! Hee! Hee!

Snoorrrtttt!

"Now it's time for your vaccination," said Dr Polar Bear.
"Do you know why we have vaccinations, Peppa?"
Peppa put her hand up. "Yes! They stop us from getting ill,
and that helps the people around us, too."

"That's right," said Dr Polar Bear, impressed. "Sometimes vaccinations are given as a little spray in your nose . . . and sometimes as a tiny pinprick in your arm."

Peppa held Teddy as Dr Polar Bear gave
her the vaccination. It was very quick.
"Well done, Peppa," said Dr Polar Bear.
"Would you like a sticker now?"

"Oooh! Yes, please!" squealed Peppa,
jumping up. "I love stickers."
"Me, too," said Dr Polar Bear, smiling.

"Are there any questions you want to ask me
before you go, Mummy Pig?" said Dr Polar Bear.
"No thank you, Doctor," replied Mummy Pig.

"I have a question!" cried Peppa. "Have you had your vaccination, Dr Polar Bear?"

"Yes, Peppa," said Dr Polar Bear.

"Good," said Peppa. "Then you can have a sticker, too!"

Peppa loves getting stickers from the doctor.
Everyone loves getting stickers from the doctor!